SHOOTING FOR THE MOON

The Amazing Life and Times of
ANNIE OAKLEY

by STEPHEN KRENSKY
Illustrated by BERNIE FUCHS

MELANIE KROUPA BOOKS

FARRAR, STRAUS AND GIROUX • NEW YORK

For Joan,
who is always on target
—S.K.

For Esme
—B.F.

ACKNOWLEDGMENTS

Many thanks to Bess M. Edwards and the Annie Oakley Foundation
for their help and encouragement, especially for providing access to Annie's personal diaries.

Photograph of Annie Oakley courtesy of the Denver Public Library, Western History Collection.

THE OLD KENTUCKY RIFLE hung in plain sight over the fireplace. It belonged to Jacob Mozee, a poor Ohio farmer. Nobody else was supposed to use the rifle—not his wife, Susan, or his seven children, including little Phoebe Ann, whom everyone called Annie.

It was 1865. The Mozees lived in a two-room cabin with a dirt floor. The children had few clothes to wear or toys to play with, but there was plenty to do. Everyone helped out—tending crops and milking Pink, the family cow. Even five-year-old Annie gathered eggs and picked up apples that had fallen from the trees. If a family wasn't prepared, winter could be deadly.

One snowy morning, Annie's father set out to take their corn and wheat to the mill fourteen miles away. As the temperature dropped, a fierce wind whipped the snow into a blizzard. Night fell while Annie and her family waited and waited. But her father didn't return.

Then, around midnight, they heard the squeak of wagon wheels. There, with the reins tied around his neck and wrists—for his hands were frozen and he could not use them—was Annie's father. He sat still as a statue in the howling wind, unable to speak. "We all carried him in," Annie remembered, "leaving the wagon right there until it was dug out of the snow two days later."

They cared for him through the long winter months, but it did no good. He died before spring came.

Without Jacob, the family struggled even more. Only Pink was content, chewing grass or licking baby Huldie's toes. But when Annie's older sister, Mary, caught sick and died, Pink had to be sold. "How we cried when Pink left us," Annie remembered. "But we had to pay for Mary's funeral and doctor bills."

At least Annie could help, catching rabbits and quail in the woods. "I busied myself with traps made from the heaviest cornstalks, laid up like a log house and tied together by strings."

Her father's rifle still hung over the fireplace, though, and Annie wondered if she could use it to hunt. One day when she was eight, she and her brother dragged the heavy gun down and filled it with "enough powder to kill a buffalo."

Outside, she leaned it against the porch railing. "Suddenly, a cottontail bobbed up. I took aim. What a kick that old gun had. It flew right back at my nose. I got the rabbit, but my nose was broken."

That night little sparks of gunpowder sputtered on the hearth. As Annie's mother swept them up, she looked Annie right in the eye. "The next time you must have the gun, Annie, ask me, and we'll not spill so much powder."

But shooting rabbits couldn't solve the family's problems. Things became so difficult that Annie was sent to stay with family friends, the Edingtons, who ran the county poor farm. Cooped up inside, Annie went to school and sewed dresses for other girls.

A few weeks later a stranger appeared. He wanted a young girl to help out at home with his wife and new baby. Annie would suit them just fine. And if she wished, Annie could spend her free time hunting and trapping around their land.

Tempted by his kind words, Annie decided to go.

But soon she found herself treated badly. She called the man and his wife "the Wolves," for they had hidden their true selves at first, like wolves in sheep's clothing. "I got up at four in the morning, got breakfast, milked the cows, washed the dishes, skimmed milk, fed the calves and pigs, pumped water for the cattle, fed the chickens, rocked the baby, weeded the garden, got dinner—and *then* could go hunting and trapping."

For two years Annie suffered. The Wolves didn't let her write to her mother. Once they even locked her outside in the snow to teach her to obey them. But as Annie got older, she got braver. One day, when she was about twelve, she just ran off. She made her way to the train station and borrowed money for a ticket home.

Everyone was shocked to hear the truth about the Wolves, but at least Annie was safe. When she returned to her mother's house, she was determined to help provide food for the family. And that meant she could now spend time in the place she loved most—the woods.

But Annie was tired of being poor. At age fifteen she traveled to the Katzenberger brothers' grocery store in the small town of Greenville with an idea. Would they buy all the small game she could ship them?

They certainly would. So Annie invested in "traps, powder, shot and coppertoed boots." Back home she studied the woods, set her traps, and hunted. With her keen eye and steady hand she rarely missed. Then she wrapped her game in bunches of six and twelve and sent it by coach to the Katzenberger brothers, who sold it to fancy hotels as far away as Cincinnati. It was said that Annie's game was especially popular because she shot it cleanly through the head. That meant that restaurant customers didn't have to pick buckshot out of their meal when they ate.

While Annie never shot more than she needed and was proud that she was "not what they'd call a game hog," her business was a big success. In a short time, she was able to support her family and even pay off the mortgage on her mother's home.

When Annie was twenty, she entered a special match shooting clay pigeons. Her opponent, Frank Butler, was a well-known professional sharpshooter. Annie heard that when he first caught sight of her, he asked, "Who is this country girl?" She would show him soon enough.

The two met in an open field.

"Pull!" called out Mr. Butler.

The first clay pigeon was launched. He hit it dead-on.

Now Annie tried. "My knees were shaking. I lined the gun up, then, dropping it quickly below the elbow, called, 'Pull!'"

Another hit.

Twenty-three times they went back and forth. The crowd drew closer as dust from the exploding clay clouded the air.

On his last shot, Frank Butler missed. But Annie didn't.

Afterward Mr. Butler helped Annie back into her carriage. She was impressed. Here was a kind man—and a good loser. As Frank Butler continued his travels, he and Annie exchanged many letters. Soon they fell in love and married.

Annie took to the road with her new husband. Growing up poor had taught her to watch her pennies. She got used to traveling in dusty trains and sleeping in boardinghouses.

At first Annie just watched her husband perform. But one night Frank couldn't hit his targets, and he asked her to take over. Only five feet tall, in her long dress and starched white collar, Annie hardly looked like a sharpshooter.

"I went through one miss, but scored the second shot . . . knocking a small cork from the bottom of a wine glass which was held upside down in Mr. Butler's hand," she said.

The crowd cheered. Everyone was used to seeing women cook and sew and clean house. A woman who could shoot like Annie was a rare sight indeed.

Soon Annie and Frank were performing together. Her stunts became more and more daring. In one trick, she held a mirror in one hand and shot back over her shoulder at a target. In another, she was able to snuff out the flame of a burning candle with a single shot from her rifle.

She even did a trick with her pet poodle, George—shooting an apple off his head. When the apple exploded, George always caught the largest piece in his mouth.

As their fame grew, Annie picked out a stage name for herself. Perhaps she got the idea from the Cincinnati neighborhood of Oakley. Whatever its source, "Annie Oakley" had a nice ring to it . . . so Annie Oakley she became.

Soon she and Frank joined a circus, performing with clowns, two hippos, and Emperor, the giant elephant. But Annie dreamed of being more than just a supporting player. She wanted to take center stage.

Annie got her chance with Buffalo Bill's Wild West Show. Buffalo Bill Cody was a former Pony Express rider, buffalo hunter, and army scout. When Annie met him, she could see he was worried that she might be too small and delicate for the job. So she made Buffalo Bill an offer—if she didn't measure up after a three-day audition, she and Frank would pack their bags and be gone.

To build her strength, Annie practiced shooting glass balls with a shotgun. From fifteen yards away she shattered 4,777 out of 5,000 balls in one nine-hour stretch. Weeks of further practice left her ready and able. When her audition came, she passed it with flying colors.

The Wild West Show featured stagecoach ambushes, mock battles, and buffalo hunts. Dozens of cowboys and Indians took part, including the famous Sioux leader Sitting Bull. The chief had seen Annie perform before. He called her *Machin Chilla Watonya Cecilla*, meaning "My daughter, Little Sure Shot."

Annie was honored. Most people were angry with the Indians for fighting to defend their lands. But Annie insisted that Sitting Bull "fought justly, for his people had been driven from their God-given inheritance."

The hustle and bustle surrounding Annie suited her nicely. "The travel and the early parades were hard, but I was happy. A crowned queen was never treated with more reverence than was I by those whole-souled western boys."

Annie was becoming famous. In interviews she never bragged about her talent. Her guns spoke for themselves. But she never forgot her poor background. She gave away show tickets to children, especially orphans, because she knew what it was like to lose a parent herself.

In 1886, the show settled in for a long stay in New York City. There, long lines of devoted fans, many of them poor, often waited hours for the doors of the old Madison Square Garden to open. Annie recalls that even in freezing weather, her fans never failed to remove their hats when she passed.

Annie continued to think up new tricks to delight her audiences. Charging at full speed on her horse, she slid down headfirst from her Western sidesaddle and untied a handkerchief placed right above her galloping horse's hoof. Then, still upside down, she scooped up more handkerchiefs and her whip from the ring and waved them at the cheering crowd.

In another trick, she gracefully stood up on her horse as it circled the ring. Then she raised her rifle, aimed at Frank—and shot playing cards right out of his hand.

But Annie always saved her most difficult trick for last. It involved a rifle, five shotguns on a table, and eleven glass balls. First Annie took the rifle and held it upside down. Across the way, Frank was ready. At Annie's signal, he tossed up a ball.

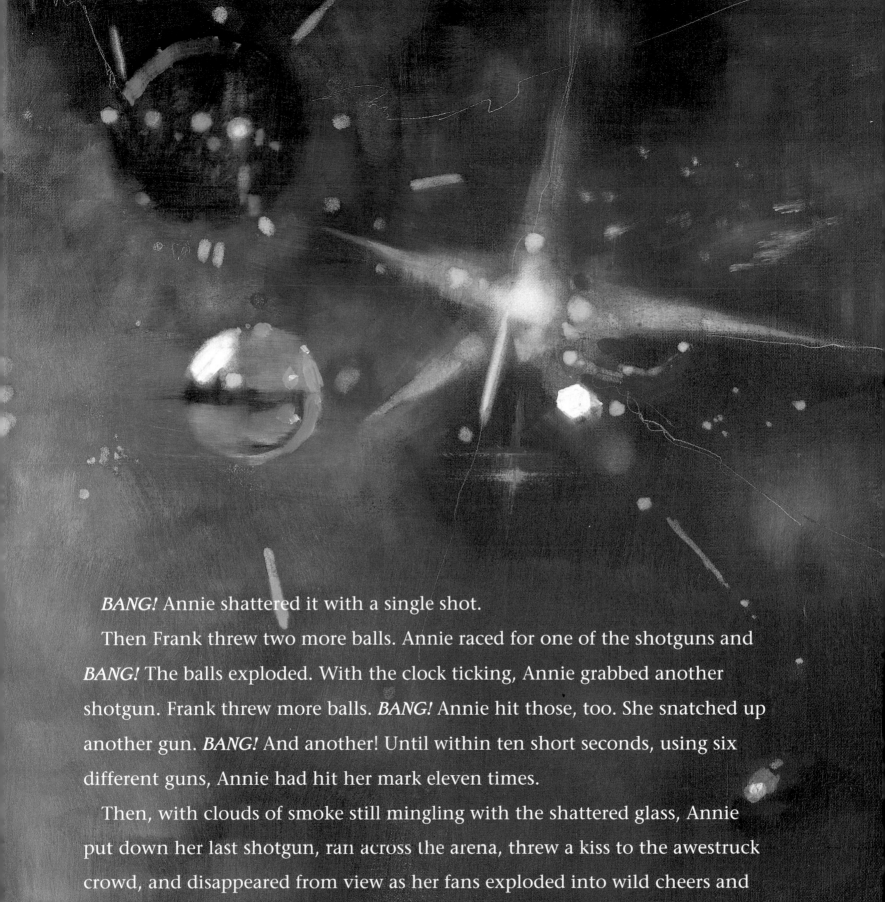

BANG! Annie shattered it with a single shot.

Then Frank threw two more balls. Annie raced for one of the shotguns and *BANG!* The balls exploded. With the clock ticking, Annie grabbed another shotgun. Frank threw more balls. *BANG!* Annie hit those, too. She snatched up another gun. *BANG!* And another! Until within ten short seconds, using six different guns, Annie had hit her mark eleven times.

Then, with clouds of smoke still mingling with the shattered glass, Annie put down her last shotgun, ran across the arena, threw a kiss to the awestruck crowd, and disappeared from view as her fans exploded into wild cheers and loud applause.

On her best days, Annie said, she "drew a streak of greased lightning" as she hit her targets. But even on those few occasions when she missed, she never lost her confidence. She had been shooting for the moon, for success and respect, her whole life—and now she had it at last.

"Aim at a high mark and you will hit it," was Annie's motto. "No, not the first time, nor the second, and maybe not the third. But keep on aiming and keep on shooting. Finally you'll hit the bull's-eye of success, for only practice will make you perfect."

A FTER PERFORMING IN NEW YORK, Annie Oakley continued with the Wild West Show both in America and Europe. At one performance in Paris, the king of Senegal asked Annie if she would accompany him back to Africa. He wanted her to protect his villagers from man-eating wild beasts. (Luckily for the beasts, Annie declined.) During her travels, Annie competed as a marksman in many competitions, often with royalty. Annie was also a particular favorite at the Chicago World's Fair in 1893—as much of a draw as the Arts Palace or the first gigantic Ferris wheel.

In 1902, Annie retired from the Wild West Show. But she wasn't ready for a rocking chair just yet. She starred in a play, performing as the Western girl she knew so well. She wrote magazine articles on the sport of shooting, including a booklet on gun safety—which she always stressed, saying, "I have no patience with a careless shooter, however brilliant a shot that person might be." During World War I, she toured the country to raise money for the Red Cross. She never tired of shooting. At sixty-two, she could still smash a hundred clay pigeons without a miss.

Annie was born just as the Civil War was about to begin. In many states women were still legally considered the property of men, but as Annie grew up, the country grew with her. By the turn of the century, the role of women was changing. More and more women were demanding the right to vote. Annie's great success competing in a sport considered off-limits to women helped change people's ideas about what women could and couldn't do. Without intending to, she broke barriers in the field of sports, becoming recognized as one of the first great female sports figures.

Annie Oakley died in November 1926. As Will Rogers, the speaker and humorist, had written of her just a few months earlier, she was "the greatest woman rifle shot the world has ever produced. Nobody took her place. There was only one."